P9-DCB-963

In Two Worlds:
A Yup'ik Eskimo Family

In Two Worlds:
A Yup'ik Eskimo Family

Aylette Jenness and Alice Rivers
Photographs by Aylette Jenness

Houghton Mifflin Company
Boston   1989

979.8
J

Library of Congress Cataloging-in-Publication Data

Jenness, Aylette.
    In two worlds : a Yup'ik Eskimo family / Aylette Jenness and Alice
Rivers; photographs by Aylette Jenness.
        p.   cm.
    Bibliography: p.
    Includes index.
    Summary: Text and photographs document the life of a Yup'ik Eskimo
family, residents of a small Alaskan town on the coast of the Bering
Sea, detailing the changes that have come about in the last fifty years.
    ISBN 0-395-42797-5
    1. Eskimos—Alaska—Juvenile literature. [1. Eskimos—Alaska.
2. Indians of North America.] I. Rivers, Alice, ill. II. Title.
E99.E7J55   1989
979.8′00498—dc19   88-13887
                          CIP
                          AC

Printed in the United States of America

M 10 9 8 7 6 5 4 3 2 1

Contents

Acknowledgments

We would like to thank

the people and the teachers of Scammon Bay for their ideas and
for the photographs of them that appear here;

Leota and Mary Ann Sundown for Mary Ann's life story;

Frances Goldin, our agent, for her commitment to the book;

Matilda Welter and Susan Sherman for their caring work as
editor and designer;

Michael Moya for his painstaking printing of photographs;

Billy Rivers and Sam Bowles for their support of their hard-
working partners.

For photographs not taken by Aylette Jenness, we thank

Jonathan Jenness, pages 6, 10, 11, 15, 16, 22, 23;

James Barker of Bethel, Alaska, page 26;

the Gonzaga Collection, Yugtarvik Museum, Bethel, Alaska,
page 8.

Last

Alice thanks Aylette for coming all the way to Scammon Bay to
get information for the book.

Aylette thanks Irene and David Kaganak and their family for
their friendship and hospitality, Frank Keim for his interest
and insights, Pat Everson-Brady for a warm welcome at the
school, and Alice for being herself.

For
Bert and Mattie Rivers
Teddy and Mary Ann Sundown

Introduction

This book has grown out of an old friendship. It began when Alice was a teenager (and helped take care of Aylette's babies while Aylette was first writing about Scammon Bay). It was reborn twenty-five years later when Aylette came back to Scammon Bay (and helped take care of Alice's grandbabies for a little while).

Aylette wanted to tell this story so that people Outside — meaning outside of Alaska — could learn how Yup'ik Eskimo families live today. Alice wanted to tell the story as a record for her children, and their children, of their life.

Alice's ideas of what was important to include in the book were listed by Aylette. Conversations became tape recording sessions in which Alice, Billy, and the children talked about their lives.

They spoke to you, the reader, in English, so that those of you who don't read Yup'ik, their first language, would be able to understand. Photographs were taken, printed, and chosen. Drafts of the text were written by Aylette and edited by Alice.

And who knows, maybe in another twenty-five years, when they are both old, Alice and Aylette will write another book — about Yup'ik people in the twenty-first century. Or maybe one of Alice's daughters will write that one. Mattie? Sarah? How about it?

ALASKA

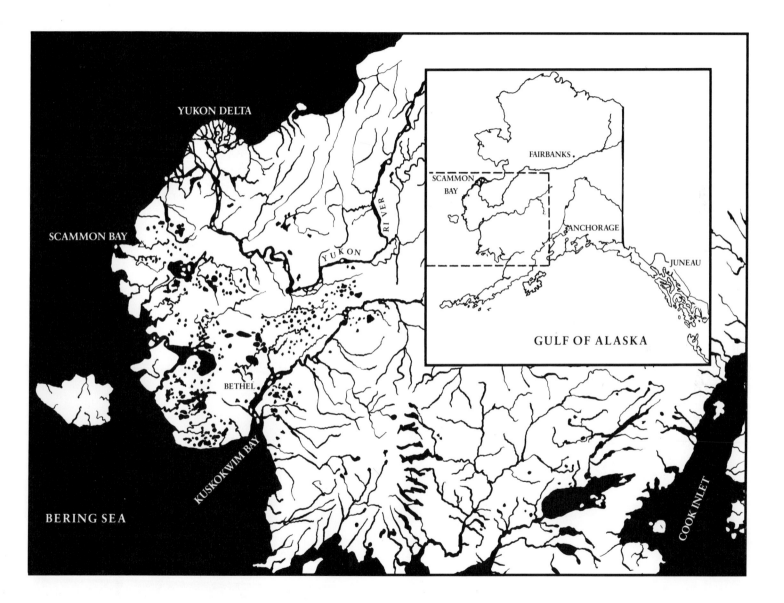

YUKON DELTA

SCAMMON BAY

BERING SEA

KUSKOKWIM BAY

BETHEL

YUKON

RIVER

FAIRBANKS

SCAMMON
BAY

ANCHORAGE

JUNEAU

GULF OF ALASKA

COOK INLET

PART I: THE PAST
Long Ago

Alice and Billy Rivers live with their children in the small town of Scammon Bay, Alaska, on the coast of the Bering Sea. They are Yup'ik Eskimos. This book is about their life today, but the story really begins long, long ago.

Alice and Billy's parents, grandparents, great-grandparents, great-great-grandparents — all their ancestors for several thousand years — have always lived here. They were part of a small group of Yup'ik Eskimos whose home was this vast area of tidal flats bordering the sea, with, inland, marshes, ponds, creeks, and rivers lacing the flat treeless tundra, broken only by occasional masses of low hills.

Each year, as the northern part of the earth tilted toward the sun, the long hours of sunlight here melted the snow, melted the sea ice, melted the rivers, melted, even, the frozen land down to the depth of a foot or so. Briefly, for a few months, birds came from the south to lay their eggs and raise their young. The fish spawned, plants grew, berries ripened. And then the earth tilted away from the sun. Days grew shorter, the sun weaker, temperatures fell. The rain turned to snow, plants withered, birds flew south. Ponds, creeks, rivers, and finally even the Bering Sea froze, and layers of snow covered the whole landscape. Fish, sea mammals, and land animals all moved beneath thick blankets of ice and snow.

The small, scattered groups of Yup'ik Eskimos knew exactly how to survive here. Living as single families, or in small groups of relatives, they moved with the seasons to catch each kind of fish, bird, or mammal when and where each was most

easily available. They harpooned the whales that migrated north along the coast in spring and south in the fall. They shot and snared birds nesting on the tundra, and they gathered the birds' eggs. They netted saltwater fish coming to lay their eggs in the rivers and creeks, and they caught freshwater fish moving beneath the ice of inland creeks. They trapped small mammals on the land for meat and for fur clothing. They knew where to find and how to catch dozens of different fish and animals for food, for clothing, even for light and heat for their small homes.

They had fire, but they didn't know how to use it to make metal. Everything they had they made themselves, with their hands, with stone, bone, or ivory tools — their many intricate snares and nets and traps, their boats and sleds, their homes and their clothing. Life was hard and precarious. Nothing was wasted.

Their mark on the land was light. Today their old sites are nearly part of the earth, not easy to see. These Yup'ik Eskimos didn't build monuments to gods or leaders. They believed that animals had spirits, and that the spirits survived the animals' death to inhabit other animals. After killing a seal, they put water in its mouth to show their caring and respect for it and to ensure that its spirit would return in the form of another seal another time. They made up stories and dances of awe, fear, and pleasure in the animals they knew so well.

They shared with each other, and no one was much better or worse off than anyone else. Families, or groups of families, had rights to certain places for hunting or fishing, but no one owned the land or its resources.

They knew no outsiders, no one different from themselves. During those hundreds and hundreds of years, their way of life changed very little. People followed in the footsteps of their ancestors, children learning from their parents the vast body of knowledge necessary for survival in this environment.

But during the last fifty years, their lives have changed enormously. And these changes are within the memory of the older people living here now.

Listen to Alice Rivers's mother, Mary Ann, describe her childhood. She speaks in Yup'ik, and one of her daughters, Leota, translates into English.

Mary Ann Remembers

"I was born, as I was told, in the late fall. My mother delivered me outside in the tundra, out in the open. My mother told me that after I was born I clutched some tundra moss and grass in my hand. I do not know why I was born outside, but it must have been because my mother was out in the tundra.

"When I was first aware of my surroundings, we lived on the other side of the mountains of Scammon Bay. The name of the place where I was born is called Ingeluk, and I think it's called this name because we are surrounded by small hills. We were the only people living in that area. We were secluded away from other people. There was my father, my mother, my two older sisters, and one older brother, and I am the youngest in the family.

"We lived in a sod house. The insides of our house had braided grass hanging on the walls as paneling. We had only one window, which was made out of dried seal guts, and it made a lot of noise when it was windy. Our floor was plain, hard, dried mud. Our beds were dried grass, piled high to keep us warm. We had no blankets. We mostly did with what we had at hand, and we used our parkas to keep us warm. I re-member we had one kettle, a small half kerosene tank for our cooking pot, and the plates we had were carved from wood by my father.

"For light, we used seal oil when we had the oil, and it

smoked a lot. Other times we had no light because we had no oil. I remember my mother cooked whitefish, and she carefully skimmed off the oil from the pot we had, and what she took out of the cooking pot we used in our oil lamp. The oil from the fish made pretty good light; it never smoked like the seal oil did. There were lots of stories being told, that's what we did during the evenings.

"Our main diet was fish, caught in my father's traps. There were times that we were really hungry. We were very poor.

Sometimes when we woke up in the morning, we had nothing at all to eat.

"We didn't have any kind of bread. We did not know what coffee and tea were.

"I saw my first white man when we were traveling by our skin boat. I did not know who he was, but later on I was told that the white man was trading goods for fur or skins. Maybe I was fifteen years old when I saw an airplane.

"I liked the life we used to live a long time ago, but we were always in need of something. I would say we live in comfort now. I don't go in hunger now. I say both lives I led were good, and I like both."

Mary Ann grew up and married a man who lived nearby, Teddy Sundown. They began to raise their family in Keggatmiut, as Scammon Bay is known in Yup'ik. It was a good site, and a number of families settled there. They built their small log houses on the lower slope of a range of hills that rose out of the flat tundra. A clear stream, racing down the hillside, flowed into the river that wound along the base of the hills, and finally emptied into a wide, shallow bay of the Bering Sea. Mary Ann and Teddy still moved to seasonal camps to fish, trap, and hunt, but as the village grew, they began to spend more and more of the year there.

The United States government set up a school in Scammon Bay and hired a Yup'ik teacher. All of the children were expected to attend school.

Missionaries had come to convert the people from their traditional religion, and the village was divided between Catholics and Protestants. Two churches were built.

Alice was the fourth child born to Mary Ann and Teddy. Here she is at the age of ten, standing on the far right of her family. She speaks of growing up in Scammon Bay.

Alice Remembers

"Our home was a one-room building. Our beds were together — Mom and Dad's bed and our bed. All of us kids slept together in one bed. No table — the tables came later on. We used to eat sitting on the floor, Eskimo way. Mom used to cook bread on top of the stove, 'cause there was no oven. To me it used to be the best bread I've eaten. Then as I grew older, we got a stove and oven, and she started baking bread.

"We ate bread, birds, dried herrings, clams, mussels, fish — boiled and frozen — seals, mink, muskrats. There were two stores. We bought shortening, flour, tea, coffee — just what we needed.

"We were always together. We'd go to church every morning. Mom would wake us up early, we'd go to mass. We never used to be lazy, we used to just go, get up and go, get up to a real cold morning, and by the time we were home, the house would be nice and warm.

"Right after church we used to go straight to school, all of us. I remember that learning to write my name was the hardest

thing. I was maybe about six. We had Eskimo teachers. It was one room, and everything was there.

"After school, we'd have lots of things to do — bringing some wood in, dishes to wash, house to clean, babies to watch, water to pack. We had aluminum pails with handles. We used to run over to the stream and pack water until we had what we needed. In the winter we had to keep one hole in the ice open the whole winter. This was one of the things I used to do with my sisters, not only me.

"Planes came in maybe once a week with mail. We didn't know about telephones. We had a radio, just for listening. I think we listened to one station all the time. No TV.

"The teachers had a short-wave radio. If someone got sick, they would report us to the hospital. They would give us medication or send us to the hospital in Bethel."

Alice Grown Up

By the time Alice was an adult, Scammon Bay was a village of a hundred and fifty people, with twenty-five log and frame homes. For transportation, each family had a dog sled and team, and a boat for use in summer.

The government began to take a larger role in the Yup'ik villages. A new school was built, with living quarters for non-Eskimo teachers from outside of Alaska. Children were taught a standard public elementary school curriculum, which had little reference either to their own lives or to what they knew and didn't know about life outside Scammon Bay. They were forbidden to speak Yup'ik in school, in the belief that this would help them to learn English, and that learning English was very important.

A postmaster was hired from among the village men, and a custodian for the school. A health aide was trained, and a small clinic built and stocked. More planes came to Scammon Bay, and it became easier to fly someone needing hospital care out — as long as the weather was good.

Government money became available for low-income families and for the elderly and disabled. There were few opportunities to earn cash, but almost all of the men in Scammon Bay were able to earn *some* money by hunting or trapping seals, mink, muskrats, and beaver and selling the skins to be made into luxury fur coats outside of Alaska. In summer they netted salmon in the river mouths north of Scammon Bay and sold this valuable fish to processors, who marketed it throughout the United States as smoked fish, or lox.

Each summer a freighter came up the coast from Seattle, Washington, with supplies for the villages. Everyone began to buy more factory-made goods. Some families bought stoves that burned fuel oil instead of relying on brush wood they cut nearby. Some bought windmills, which produced enough electricity for one or two light bulbs in their homes. Some bought snowmobiles, which enabled them to travel farther than they could by dog team to hunt and trap, but which, unlike dogs, required money for fuel and new parts.

And for the first time in the long history of the Yup'ik Es-kimos, some people began to travel away from their homeland. Some teenagers went to boarding school in the state of Washington. Some men went to National Guard training, and some

families moved away permanently, settling in Alaskan towns and cities, or even as far away as Oregon and California.

But most remained in Scammon Bay, and some new Yup'ik people came to live there from other towns.

Alice speaks of her life at this time: "Billy moved to Scammon Bay from Hooper Bay, and after a while we got married. We did a lot of things that first-married couples do all over the world. Married couples have secrets of their own!

"We didn't have a Snow Go, but in those years we had a dog team, which we depended on very much for travel. I didn't go out every day, but toward springtime, that's the time I'd get to go a lot. We'd go tomcod fishing, rabbit hunting, ptarmigan hunting, geese hunting, seal hunting, go get wood, go to spring camp. We used to go out hunting a lot. I'm an expert at shooting ptarmigans. Billy taught me how to shoot. I use a 20-gauge shotgun.

"Mattie, my oldest daughter, was born when I was twenty-four. And then, maybe a year and a half later, Bernie was born. When Bernie was born, I adopted her out to Billy's sister, and ever since then she's been raised up by them. Then I had Oscar. They were all born in the hospital in Bethel. But I don't like having babies in the hospital because you get bothered too much. That's what made me decide to have the others at home. My mom, and my aunt, Agnes Henry, and Gemma, the health aide, helped me. I knew exactly what to do. The last ones, Jacob, Abraham, Isaac, Sarah, and Billy Junior, were like the other pregnancies, no problem. My mom had told me to be active, not lazy, not sit around. If you do things slow, your labor will be slow. If you do things fast, right away, it will be a fast labor.

"After the last one, I decided to quit having kids. There was too much work to do besides my job — I always worked, from the time Mattie was small, as the school cook. I went over to Bethel to the hospital, and I had them do a small surgery so I wouldn't have more kids.

"So I had eight kids altogether. As the years went by, my daughters grew, my sons grew."

PART II: NOW

Alice's life today is both very similar to that of her mother at the same age — and very different. Scammon Bay has grown and changed in many ways.

There are three hundred and fifty people in Scammon Bay now, living in fifty-six houses. Most of the old log homes are now used for storage, and many people, like the Riverses, have new houses provided by the government at low cost. A dish antenna relays television to all the homes. Satellite transmission enables families to make telephone calls anywhere in the world. Huge storage tanks hold fuel to run an electric generator that provides enough power for each home to have all the lights that people want. A water and sewage disposal system required building a water treatment plant and a lagoon on the tundra for waste water. The dump, full of cans, plastic, fuel drums, and broken machinery, is a reminder of the difficulty of disposing of modern trash.

For some years the state government made a great deal of money from taxes on oil found in Alaska, and this money paid for many of the modern conveniences in Scammon Bay and other rural towns. An airstrip was built so that planes could land more easily at all times of the year; it is regularly plowed in winter. Three small planes a day fly into Scammon Bay, bringing everything from cases of soft drinks to boxes of disposable diapers and, of course, the mail. A huge new gym has been built, and a new clinic, a preschool center, town offices, and a post office. The school is now run by the state, not the federal government, and goes all the way through the twelfth grade. In recent years, as oil tax money has decreased, some services have been cut back; this will probably continue.

In spite of the changes, the traditional pattern of living from the land is still powerful. This can be seen most clearly as people move to seasonal camps during the summer months.

Fish Camp/*Neqlirik*

On rocky Bering Sea beaches south of the village, herring come in immense schools to lay their eggs, and many families move there to fish for several weeks. Alice and Billy leave Scammon Bay with the children as soon as school is out for the summer.

Alice says, "Billy goes first and sets up our camp — tent, blankets, bed, clothes, pots and pans for cooking, and our grub. Then we go, maybe the third week in May. We pick spring greens, go hunting, take walks. We eat fish and fresh geese. It never gets dark when we're out camping, and it's fun."

Billy and other fishermen catch the herring in gill nets, both for their own use and to sell. Here the old ways and the new meet; Yup'ik Eskimos have been catching herring and drying them for winter food for hundreds of years, but it is only recently that they have been able to sell them for cash.

Billy sells his catch — as much as twenty thousand pounds of herring in a good year — to huge Japanese fish processing boats that wait out to sea. Prevented by law from fishing close to the coast of the United States, the Japanese buy the catch of Americans. The herring eggs are a great delicacy for the Japanese, who will pay very high prices for this special-occasion food. Most of the rest of the fish is ground up to make fertilizer.

Scammon Bay people still dry large numbers of herring for the winter, just as they have for hundreds of years. Split open, cleaned, and hung up to dry, the fish become a good-tasting, chewy, oily, protein-rich food that can last all winter. The fish that aren't caught in the nets lay their eggs on seaweed along the shores. The seaweed, dried, is also a traditional favorite food of Scammon Bay people. Soaked in water during the winter, it tastes fresh at a time when no fresh vegetables are available.

When the herring run is finished, people get ready to go north up the coast to the mouths of the rivers where salmon enter to lay their eggs. This is another chance to earn money. And Alice will dry a lot of salmon for the family's own use.

Berry Picking/*Iqvaq*

Returning to the village again, summer's traditional bounty is not quite over. Alice describes one of her favorite activities. "About August we prepare for picking salmonberries. After they're ripe, we go out nearly every day, all of us. We freeze enough to last all winter. After salmonberries we pick a little blueberries, and after blueberries, right into the crowberries, and then a little bit of cranberries."

Here they go by boat up the river that borders Scammon Bay and scatter out across the tundra to pick salmonberries. The younger kids eat as much as they save, but everyone contributes to the buckets they will take home.

Seal Hunting/*Qamigaq*

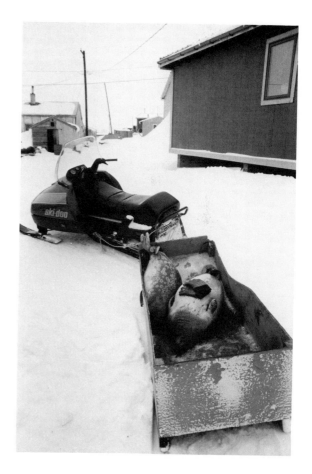

During the summer and fall Billy takes his boat into the river mouth and further out into the Bering Sea to catch seals. He is a good shot and a very successful hunter. He uses the teachings of his ancestors in figuring out when, where, and how to look for the fast-moving, wary seals. And he uses a modern high-speed rifle and a boat with a powerful outboard motor to catch them.

He often catches enough to provide fresh meat and warm fur skins for many of Alice's relatives — her parents, her sisters, and their children, in the traditional way of sharing so that no one goes without.

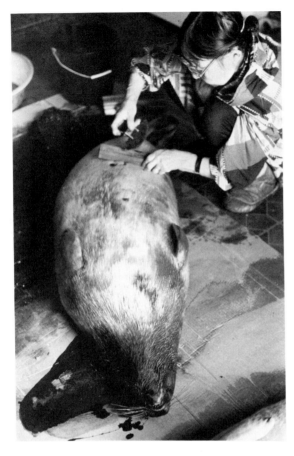

Alice's mother, Mary Ann, now sixty-five years old, is still the most expert in the family at butchering seals. When Billy catches several on one trip, she does the cutting for the whole family.

Using a traditional curved knife, she quickly slits the seal's skin along its belly, and peels the coat of fur away from the thick layer of fat underneath. The skin will be stretched, dried, scraped, and tanned to make into warm winter boots for the family. Many people in Scammon Bay wear factory-made snowmobile boots, but for really cold weather most people still

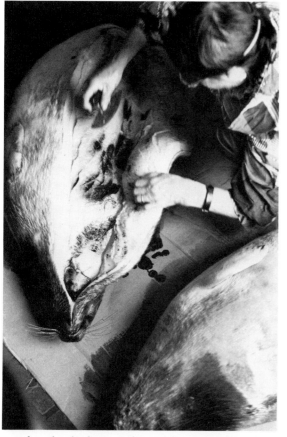

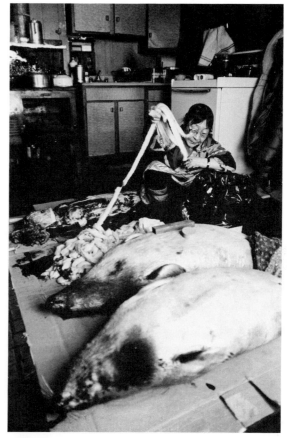

prefer the lightweight, soft, grass-lined sealskin boots that have been worn here for generations.

The layer of fat beneath the seal's skin acts as insulation to keep the seal warm in the icy Arctic waters. The fat is no longer used for fuel in the seal oil lamps Mary Ann remembers from her childhood, but it is still appreciated as a delicious oil to eat with dried fish. No part of the seal is wasted. Any meat not cooked tonight will be frozen for the future; the liver and the cleaned intestines will be eaten, too. Nothing is left except the bones, and a few internal organs, like the lungs, that people don't like to eat; these will be given to the village dogs.

Home Life/*Enunarmi*

At home, Alice prepares the seal meat for cooking; everyone likes this fresh food. As members of the family come indoors at the end of the day, they sit down to eat at the table in their new house.

The Rivers house today is far different from the house of Alice's childhood, and far far different from that of her

mother's childhood. Alice says, "I think that when I was a kid, it was fun because I was free. Now I have my own family — husband to take care of, kids to take care of. But it's easier now, 'cause I have a washer, a dryer, I have hot water, I have a shower, I have a tub. There's four bedrooms, a stove, a furnace, a refrigerator, a freezer."

And Alice needs this big new home, for the family is large. Alice and Billy's second daughter, Bernie (given in adoption to Billy's childless sister, in a tradition which enables all families to raise children) has herself had a baby Alice and Billy are raising. Mattie has also had a child, so the Rivers household includes two much-loved little boys — Adam and Isaiah.

In this new home Mattie has her own bedroom, where she can iron and hang up her clothes. Here she can give her friend a home permanent and talk in privacy. The younger kids don't mind sharing bedrooms, and they love having a bathroom with a tub, the first one they've had.

The heart of the house is the living room, with a sofa and TV at one end, a table by the big center window, and the kitchen at the other end. Here Alice prepares the family's meals — whale meat, peanut butter sandwiches, Tang, dried fish, Rice Krispies, boiled ducks, whitefish, fried bread, popcorn, *akutag* — whatever is in season and whatever they can afford from the village store.

For a treat Alice often makes *akutag*. She says, "After you mix shortening, sugar, and fish together, then you put in salmonberries, blackberries, or raisins. That's what *akutag* means — mixing up together. It's a favorite of everybody — all Eskimos." Alice lets Sarah lick *akutag* from her fingers, while baby Isaiah looks on.

For her big family Alice makes bread at least twice a week. Sometimes she fries it, as here, and sometimes she bakes many loaves. Billy Junior and Sarah love to help, and Alice almost always lets them. The smell of fresh bread fills the house, and the kids eat it until they're full.

Occasionally the whole family gathers to watch television. Alice says, "My favorites are 'All My Children,' 'General Hospital,' and 'The Price is Right.' Billy thinks that's junk — he watches some animal movies, like 'Wild Kingdom,' and basketball, baseball. I hardly watch those things! The kids mostly watch cartoons most of the time. And they watch some movies that they like.

"To me, television gives the kids some dirty ideas. That's how the kids learn. If they watch a movie that I don't want them to watch, they might imitate it when they go out of the house, telling their friends what they saw. I don't let them watch restricted movies, it's something that we tell them not to watch. We tell them that things like that aren't good for them."

Taking care of this big family isn't always easy, but to Billy and Alice it's the most important thing in the world. Alice says, "Having teenager kids, it's kind of hard. Especially after raising them up, and then they change their lives. The girls start noticing boys. They think it's time to get — how would I describe it — they think having boyfriends is exciting, they want to be with them a lot.

"When our two oldest girls had babies, we decided that we were going to raise them as our own, since the girls are too young. They wouldn't care for them the way we took care of them, 'cause there are so many things going on, like dances and games, and they want to be there.

"At first, I used to be mad, and in a way I wished that I hadn't taken the babies. I didn't want to go back to getting up at night, changing diapers, all that work. But as the babies grew

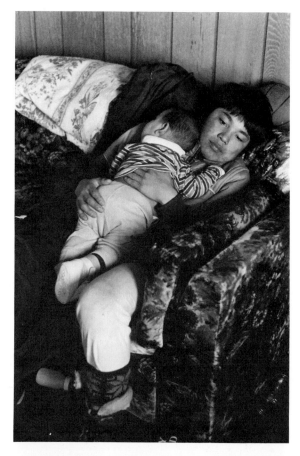

older, when they started to smile, it changed; I found out how precious they were.

"Before Adam and Isaiah were born, the other kids thought it wouldn't be good to have a baby at home. But after they were born, the kids were happy to have them, Adam and Isaiah. It makes me feel good to have the kids loving a baby again. Even the youngest one, Billy Junior. But sometimes he still misses being a baby, the baby of the family!

"Billy always talked about adopting kids. He always wanted to raise more. But me, I'm a different person, I think having too many kids is a lot of work even though it's good for men to have kids around. So that's how we decided about our first grandsons — that we'd raise them up as our own. But these two are the last ones I'm going to take!"

School/*Elicarvik*

During the school year the family's life falls into very different patterns from those of summer. Billy begins his winter rounds of hunting and fishing, going out by snowmobile nearly every day to get food or firewood for the family. Alice goes back to work as the school cook.

Mattie takes care of the babies. She says, "I stay home most of the time with my baby and with Adam. Taking care of Isaiah is hard when he's sick. When he's good it's easy.

"I help my mom with the housework. I like helping my mom. Whenever I help her, I feel good. When I don't, I always feel funny, I think that she'll think I'm a lazybones and all that.

"Sometimes when problems come, boyfriend problems, family problems, they pile up in my head. I get depressed. It's better if I talk to my parents about my problems, instead of ignoring them. Then I feel better inside of me. Mostly, I do the same old thing every day. It never changes."

Alice is always the first one up in the morning.

"When a school day starts," she says, "I get up at five-thirty or six o'clock, make coffee, sit down and drink my coffee in the nice peaceful house, with no kids around. At six-thirty or fifteen to seven, I wake Billy Junior up so he can come with me to work. The rest I'll wake them up at seven, just before I leave.

"I go over to the high school, look at the menu, start making things. In between seven and eight we get breakfast — it's either cereal, pancakes, French toast, rolled oats, boiled eggs, with juice and milk. When there's French toast, I'll use seven or eight dozen eggs — lots of cracking eggs! While my helper does other things, I do mainly the cooking. I make a mess, she takes care of it. About thirty or forty kids eat breakfast — sometimes over fifty when there's a super breakfast. Sometimes we serve fresh oranges and apples, that's if we have them. There's bacon, sausages. Most of the time my food is yummy.

"After breakfast, I have to write up what we used — how many pounds of it, how many servings. Five or six years ago I went to Fairbanks for training. I learned all sorts of things there — baking, making salads. Here we don't worry about making salads because there's no fresh vegetables, except carrots. We get frozen peas, canned fruit, canned vegetables — that's all we get. In the meat group we get frozen pork, beef for stewing, pork chops, chicken, turkey, and some canned meat. We order it from Anchorage, and it comes by plane.

"After we clean up from breakfast, it's time to look at the lunch menu. We get it ready before my ten o'clock break. Then I go back home, see how everything is. Billy is either there or out hunting. Mattie is either washing clothes, fixing up the house, washing dishes — I let her do most of the things. Then I come back and take care of other work, like making bread."

While Alice prepares lunch for the whole school, the Rivers kids are busy in their classrooms.

Billy Junior, in the second grade, is learning to type. When the older grades got electric typewriters, the manual ones were put away. Billy's teacher had taught her own children to type when they were very young, mostly for fun. She suspected that the second graders would enjoy typing, too, and that it would be good practice in language arts. She brought the typewriters into her classroom and discovered that she was right.

Billy says proudly, "I've already finished typing one book, and now I'm on another. We can read any kind of books. Now I'm on a hard one."

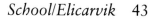

Next door, the combined third and fourth grade has a busy program. Sarah and Isaac's teacher, Tui Wi Suan, is an American whose family came originally from Asia. She is teaching about China now, and the class is learning traditional Chinese dances.

Later Sarah and Isaac's grandfather, Teddy Sundown, comes to their class. Elizabeth Kasayuli, Wi Suan's aide, and one of the few Yup'ik teachers in school, asked him to come when she was planning a social studies unit about the drought in Africa and realized that the kids had no idea what a drought was. Like the other teachers, she tries to explain school lessons through the kids' own experiences. Teddy says that while there is never a real drought in Scammon Bay, there are times when little rain falls. Then the greens that people gather for food in the summer are tough and dry, and the salmonberries are small and withered.

Teddy ends his lesson with a string game and a song, which the class loves.

Clifford Kaganak teaches Yup'ik. Traditionally, Yup'ik wasn't written, and the older people in Scammon Bay don't read it. But now all the students are learning to read and write their language. Here Clifford writes words in Yup'ik on the chalkboard, and the class practices reading and translating. The School Advisory Board in Scammon Bay wants to be sure that the Yup'ik language isn't lost as students speak English more and more of the time, and the teachers feel the same way.

Once a week, the four-year-olds in Scammon Bay spend a morning at the school so they won't be scared when it's time for them to go to kindergarten. The third and fourth graders are their teachers, under the direction of Wi Suan. At first, the little children are shy and quiet, but they love listening to stories. And Sarah and Isaac love reading. This is one of their favorite classes.

Down the hall, Jennifer Allison-Keim works with the older Rivers boys — Oscar, Jacob and Abraham. Jacob enjoys using the computers, but generally the boys would rather be out hunting and fishing — or using the school skis. Still, everyone tells them that staying in school — and doing well — is really important.

Jennifer says, "My goals are for the kids to be educated to

the point where they can protect themselves from outsiders, so if something comes their way that they have to deal with, they'll know how to weigh and measure and make decisions."

The teachers all know that the school has a great responsibility to prepare the kids for the outside world, and they also want to encourage a sense of pride in Yup'ik Eskimo culture. Some students want to go on to college after graduating from high school in Scammon Bay, and the teachers work hard to make this happen.

Around the Village/*Paqetaq*

After school Alice often goes to the store to buy groceries —
Tang, peanut butter, jelly, sometimes crackers or cookies. Isaac
likes to go with her, and when Alice gives him some change, he
stops off at the Royal Igloo, a village recreation center, to play
a video game.

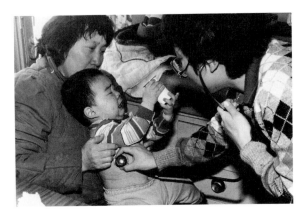

Back at the house, Alice's work continues. Now the babies are sick. Isaiah's throat is sore, and Alice feeds him milk from a dropper so he won't have to suck on a bottle. He started taking medicine a couple of days ago, and his fever is down. But now Adam feels hot and is coughing a lot. Alice and Billy decide to take him to the clinic.

At the clinic, the aide, Betty George, examines him. She'll report the illness to the doctor in Bethel, who will prescribe medicine. Alice says wryly, "When the babies are sick, we can't get any housework done, we just have to take care of them."

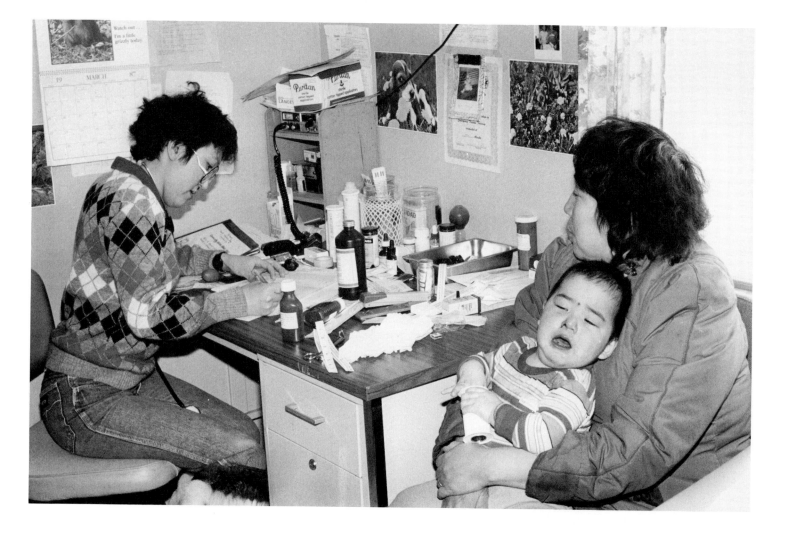

When Alice is home, Mattie is usually free to go out. She checks the mail at the post office, finding a magazine in her family's box — *Better Homes and Gardens;* this will be fun to look at.

Returning to the house, she carefully ices letters onto a cake she's baked for the Women's Annual Basketball Tournament, in which she will be playing. Then, hearing the faint sound of the late afternoon plane coming in, she hurries down to the airstrip at the edge of the village. She's happy to meet an old friend, who's flying in for the tournament from one of the two competing villages.

The tournament is held in the huge town gym, which has just been completed. Heating it takes so much fuel oil that it is used only when there is a big athletic event. Many people, from babies to grandparents, come to watch the game — and Mattie plays her hardest.

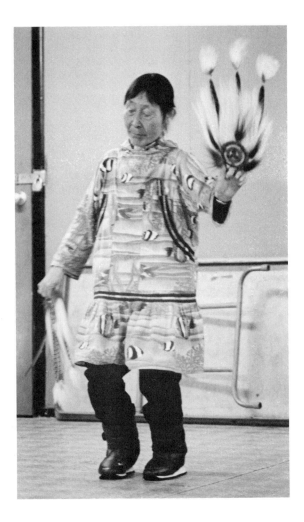

All during the years when there was no dancing, it remained in people's minds. Now the elders are teaching dancing and drumming to their children and grandchildren. Many of these dances tell stories of animals and birds through the movements of the dancers and their dance fans. Teddy Sundown plays the drums for dances nearly every week, and Mary Ann dances each time. They are happy to be passing this on to the teenagers and the little kids.

On the other side of the village, another activity is taking place — one as ancient among Yup'ik people as basketball tournaments are new. Traditional Eskimo dancing, disapproved of by the white missionaries who came to Scammon Bay long ago, is now in full swing again.

On the Tundra/*Marraq*

The end of each school week marks the beginning of two days of hunting and fishing for the whole Rivers family.

Alice says, "On the weekends, we get to go traveling with Billy. Usually we decide what we're going to do ahead of time, what's going to happen. Like if we want to go fishing, we go fishing, or hunting ptarmigans. We're out most of the day Saturday doing this and that."

This is where Billy becomes the teacher, training the kids in both the oldest methods of hunting and fishing, and the newest. Since the children spend so much time in school, this is an important time for them to learn how to survive as Eskimos.

"I teach my boys the way I've been taught, the way my dad taught me. What I think that's wrong, I try to do it better than my dad. And when I make a mistake, I try to correct it to my boys, so they'll do it better than I did.

"I start taking them out as soon as they're old enough — like in the boat, when they're old enough to sit down and take care of themselves. I tell them little things like taking the anchor out, putting the anchor back up. As soon as they understand our words, we teach them from there. If they show you something that they know, you'll know they learned it — and then they can start doing it by themselves.

"Each one of them that goes with me, I talk to them, I tell them about little things — what's dangerous, what's not dangerous. I tell them about melting ice — even though it looks good on the surface, some places you can't see when it's covered with snow, it's thin. That's where they fall through. I teach them what thin ice looks like, and how it looks when it's safe.

"Oscar's been going with me first, 'cause he's the oldest one, then Jacob. One of them will know more, the one that pays attention more, just like in school. The one that doesn't listen, or doesn't pay attention, he'll make more mistakes or get more scolding.

"Oscar was about seven or eight when I first let him shoot a gun. He got his first seal when he was maybe eight or nine. In the boat I did the driving, and I had him do the shooting. He got a young mukluk that was a baby in springtime. He shot it, and after he shot it, he looked at me, looked back, and he smiled. 'I catch it.'"

Oscar remembers this very clearly. He says, "My grandpa divided the seal up in circles and gave it to the old people." This is the traditional Yup'ik way of sharing a boy's first catch with the elders, still carried on, though motorboats have replaced kayaks, and rifles are used in place of thrown harpoons.

Going Needlefishing/*Quarruulgsuk*

The Rivers family now owns two snowmobiles, and all the older kids drive them, even ten-year-old Isaac. But even though they no longer need dogs for transportation, they still keep a team for dog sled races. And feeding eight big dogs means they must net about two hundred pounds of needlefish every week.

Needlefish, or sticklebacks, each one just an inch or two long, move in immense schools — up to a mile in length — beneath the ice of the shallow tidal rivers and creeks that lace the flat land around Scammon Bay. It takes an experienced person to know where to find them in the expanse of snow-covered tundra.

Billy says, "Oscar and Jacob could go out by themselves, but they still don't know how to find the needlefish — the beginning of the schools, and the end.

"So I go out with them, show them how to make the net hole in the ice, with an ice pick, make sure it's the right length, make sure which way the current's going, which way to face their net. You always face the current, in either direction — in incoming tide, in outgoing tide, always face the net in that direction — 'cause these small fish go with the current."

The ice may be as deep as four feet, so cutting a trench is hard, hot work. The boys and Billy take turns, and when the

slot is done, they lower the net down to the bottom of the creek, where it bells out and catches fish as they swim slowly with the current.

On a warm day like this, just below freezing, it's easy to stay out on the tundra until they have a heavy sack of fish. Half an hour trip by snowmobile, and they are back in the village. The hungry dogs get a shovelful each of needlefish.

Hooking for Tomcods/*Iqallruarsuk*

Everyone likes to go tomcod fishing downriver from the village, and the older boys can do this by themselves. Jacob could go along the tundra at the base of the hills, but he likes to take the snowmobile high up on the steep slopes and race down again.

By the time he gets to the place where the tomcods are running, several people are there already, and even a couple of
dogs. Finding a hole that someone used the previous day, he
quickly chips loose the ice covering it and lowers his line with

an unbaited hook in the water. The tomcods, running in big
schools, are attracted to the lure — a bit of red felt and a shiny

metal bottle cap — and bite at it. Watching the dark shapes in the water, Jacob jerks his line up at exactly the right moment. He hooks each tomcod lightly and flips it out onto the ice.

He will return to the village with twenty or thirty fish — a good contribution of food for the whole family.

Checking the Blackfish Trap/*Can'qiirsuk*

When they can, Alice and Billy like to go out alone. Leaving Mattie in charge of the younger children, they travel far out across the tundra to a distant creek where Billy has set a trap for blackfish.

Alice says, "I couldn't even find the blackfish traps if I went alone. I wouldn't even know where they are. It takes an expert to find blackfish traps. If I go with him, I'll ask him, 'Are they here?' He'll know exactly where to find them — 'There it is.' "

Marked only with a small stick stuck in the snow, the trap rests on the creek bottom, far below the ice. Billy cuts a hole and pulls up the trap. Its inner cone, into which the fish swim, is made of wood, as all traps were traditionally. But now the outer trap is of wire — quicker to make and longer lasting.

Here Alice and Billy discover a surprise. Mixed in with the many small blackfish, still alive and wiggling, are two drowned animals. Alice says, "Sometimes muskrats get in the trap. They swim along, and then they accidentally get into blackfish traps."

Billy has also been catching many muskrats in the traps he sets for them below the ice in tundra creeks. He sells most of the furs, earning much needed cash, and these will be made into expensive coats for women Outside. But some skins are kept for family use. Alice will make warm boots, mittens, hats and parkas.

Home again, Alice sets to work on the skins. "I learned how

to skin muskrats a long time ago, from my mom. You have to cut them in between the legs to their tail, and then as you go, you turn them inside out. Then I dry the skin until it's all dry, like drying clothes. It'll take maybe a week on the stretcher."

Later she works on the skins once more. "Tanning is the next step. I soak the skin and then scrape off the outer skin and dry it off. Then I work it until it's very soft.

"It'll be a while before we decide what we want to do with them. With a few of the muskrats Billy gets, I want to make hats for the smaller kids. They're warm, they're better than knitted hats. I've been planning, but I don't know when I'll do it."

Alice tosses the half-tanned skin on top of the television set, where it makes a small picture of the Rivers's world — the importance of the family, of the traditional lifestyle, and of outside influences. The glass plaques that Mattie has given to Billy and Alice show her feelings about them. The muskrat skin is evidence of continued living off the land, as Eskimos have done right here for thousands of years. Mattie's trophy shows that basketball is now a Yup'ik game. And television, like the radio, the school, and the daily planes, brings the outside world in, and encourages Scammon Bay people to travel out.

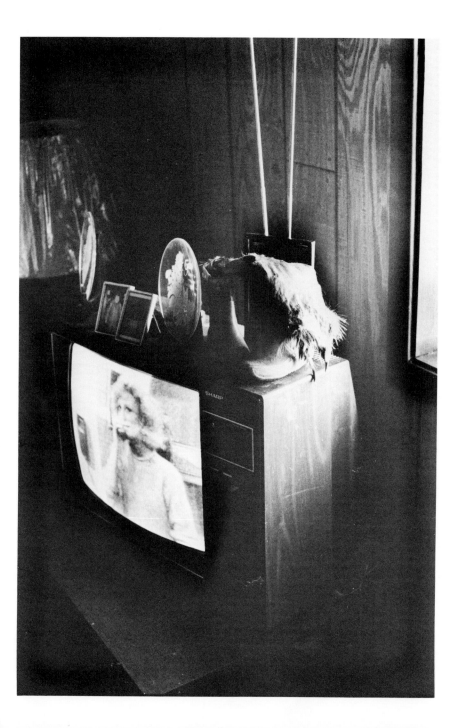

PART III: THE FUTURE

Alice and Billy know very well that life is changing fast here in Scammon Bay, and they want their children to be prepared for this.

Alice says, "When I was a kid, I used to do things with my mom. I used to watch her sew. Now I try to have Mattie knit, crochet, make things, but she thinks it's too boring. She knows how to do it, but she can't sit and look at one thing for a long time. I can't even teach her how to sew a skin. She doesn't have any patience.

"Now there's so many other things going on. In our time there was no basketball, no Igloo, hardly any dances."

Billy says, "When I was Billy Junior's age, I used to run maybe twenty or thirty times around a pond with my little wooden boat. Just run around, play with it, put mud inside of it, and run around. I'd never think of TV, it wasn't in my mind.

"Everything is not the same here in Alaska, not like before. Things are changing. Things are getting more expensive. Most of the people are depending on more jobs. I mean working, you have to have a job.

"I talk to the kids, I just say what we'd like them to do. I tell them, 'If you go to school, and be smart over there, and try to learn what you're taught, you guys will have good jobs, and good-paying jobs. I want you to have good-paying jobs, so we'll have the things that we need, anything we need'; like this I talk to them.

"I'd be happy to have them travel to see other countries, to have them learning something that's Outside — *if* they have a job. 'Cause Outside there's many people without jobs, no home. Here it's okay, as we help each other here in the villages.

"We get after the kids for not doing their homework. We want them to be more educated, more than us. I mean, learn more. I only went up to the fifth grade."

Alice agrees. She adds, "I want them to learn other ways — Outside ways. And I want them to learn our ways, too — hunting for our kind of foods. We can't have store-bought food all the time. I want them to learn both ways."

Looking down on Scammon Bay from the hill, it seems like a very small settlement, nearly lost in the huge expanse of tundra around it. From this distance it doesn't look so different from the Scammon Bay of Alice's childhood. Yet it is invisibly connected to the whole world now. And so is the Rivers family.

If You Want to Know More

Here are some books and resources about Yup'ik Eskimos and other native peoples of the Arctic, about the Arctic itself, and about the state of Alaska. Some will be easy to find, some more difficult. See what else you can discover in your library or bookstore — it's a kind of treasure hunt. You'll be in for some nice surprises.

Alexander, Bryan, and Cherry Alexander. *An Eskimo Family*. Minneapolis: Lerner Publications, 1985. Here's another Arctic family; compare them with the Rivers family.

Bruemmer, Frederick. *Seasons of the Eskimo: A Vanishing Way of Life*. Greenwich, Conn.: New York Graphic Society, 1971. An adult book with photographs for all to enjoy.

Cheney, Cora, and Ben Partridge. *Crown of the World: A View of the Inner Arctic*. New York: Dodd, Mead, 1979. Information and photographs on many aspects of the circumpolar territories, for older students.

Coles, Robert, with photographs by Alex Harris. *The Last and First Eskimos*. Boston: New York Graphic Society, 1978. A book for adults, but the older student and the careful "looker" of any age will learn a great deal about people like the Rivers family.

Elliott, Paul M. *Eskimos of the World*. New York: Messner, 1976. Drawings and lots of information about traditional life of the circumpolar peoples.

Fitzhugh, William W., and Susan Kaplan. *Inua: Spirit World of the Bering Sea Eskimo*. Washington: Smithsonian Institution Press, 1982. A book for adults based on Eskimo information and artifacts collected over a hundred years ago along the coast where the Rivers family lives; a glimpse into the worlds of their ancestors.

George, Jean Craighead. *Julie of the Wolves*. New York: Harper & Row, 1972. The exciting story of a girl surviving without her family in the Arctic.

Green, Paul. *I Am Eskimo; Aknik My Name*. Edmonds, Wash.: Alaska Northwest. Authentic stories of traditional Eskimo life.

Herbert, Wally. *Eskimos*. New York: Franklin Watts, 1976. Lots of information, mostly on traditional lifestyles, with good photographs.

Houston, James. *Long Claws: An Arctic Adventure*. New York: Atheneum, 1981.

Houston, James. *The Falcon Bow: An Arctic Legend*. New York: Macmillan, 1986. Tales from the Inuit, or Eskimo people, of Canada; look for others by the same author.

Jenness, Aylette, with photographs by Jonathan Jenness. *Dwellers of the Tundra: Life in an Alaskan Eskimo Village*. New York: Crowell-Collier, 1970. An earlier story of the world of the Rivers family.

Laycock, George. *Beyond the Arctic Circle*. New York: Four Winds, 1978. Lots of information for older students about Arctic peoples, European exploration, animal life, and the land itself.

Meyer, Carolyn. *Eskimos: Growing up in a Changing Culture*. New York: Atheneum, 1977. True-to-life fiction of Yup'ik people living near Scammon Bay.

Morgan, Lael. *Alaska's Native People*. Edmonds, Wash.: Alaska Northwest, 1979. A wonderfully rich documentary with color photographs of contemporary native life.

Newman, Gerald. *The Changing Eskimos*. New York: Franklin Watts, 1979. Easy-to-read description of the way Arctic peoples live today, illustrated with photographs.

Pitseolak, Peter. *Peter Pitseolak's Escape from Death*. New York: Delacorte, 1978.

A Canadian Inuit man's exciting account, in words and beautiful drawings, of an adventure in his life.

Rogers, Jean. *Good-bye, My Island*. New York: Greenwillow Books, 1983. The last experiences of Eskimos living on a small island off the coast of Alaska who moved to the mainland in the 1960s.

Ticasuk (Emily Ivanoff Brown). *The Roots of Ticasuk*. Edmonds, Wash.: Alaska Northwest, 1981. For young people, an Alaska native's autobiography, showing how life has changed.

Vick, Ann, ed. *The Cama-i Book*. Garden City, N.Y.: Anchor Books, 1983. Lively oral histories of native peoples, gathered by Alaska students.

You can write to the following publishers for periodicals about Arctic peoples:

The Alaska Geographic Society
Box 4 EEE
Anchorage, AK 99509
A quarterly magazine, maps, and other materials; many back issues are available through their catalog.

Alaska Native Magazine
4134 Ingra Street
Anchorage, AK 99503
A monthly devoted to the native peoples of Alaska.

Alaska Northwest Publishing Company
130 Second Avenue South
Edmonds, WA 98020
All kinds of children's and adults' books, maps, and magazines on the Arctic; write for their catalog.

Inuktitut Magazine
Indian and Northern Affairs Canada
Ottawa, KIA OH4 Canada
A free periodical about Inuit peoples of Canada.

Nunam Kitlutsisti
P.O. Box 2068
Bethel, AK 99559
Booklets, videos, curriculum units, and other materials; they have a catalog.

Tundra Drums
P.O. Box 868
Bethel, AK 99559
A weekly newspaper covering events in the area of Scammon Bay — the Yukon-Kuskokwim Delta.

Tundra Times
P.O. Box 104480
Anchorage, AK 99501
A weekly newspaper of Alaska's native peoples.

Films and videos on Alaskan Eskimo life can be obtained from the following sources:

Documentary Educational Resources
24 Dane Street
Somerville, MA 02143

EDC Distribution Center
55 Chapel Street
Newton, MA 02160

KYUK Video Productions
Box 468
Bethel, AK 99559

Index